THE FLINTSTONES

THE MOVIE STORYBOOK

ADAPTED BY WENDY S. LARSON

BASED ON A SCREENPLAY WRITTEN BY TOM S. PARKER & JIM JENNEWEIN AND STEVEN E. DE SOUZA

GROSSET & DUNLAP ◆ NEW YORK

I t was another sunny prehistoric day in Bedrock. But at the rock quarry of Slate and Co., a dark cloud was beginning to form. As workers lifted boulders one by one, Vice President Cliff Vandercave stared out from his office. He was planning to steal millions of dollars from the company.

"Somewhere down there is the waste of flesh who will make my scheme come true," he told his secretary, Miss Stone.

"WOOOOHHH!" It was the Whistlebird.

"Yabba-dabba-doo!" shouted Fred Flintstone. Sliding down his bronto-crane's tail, he leaped into the Flintmobile. After punching his time tablet, he and his best friend, Barney Rubble, set off for home.

Barney turned on K-A-V-E radio, their favorite station. It played the best music. "We're going to twitch around the clock tonight in Bedrock. Twitch, twitch," sang Fred and Barney, swaying to the beat.

"Ya know, Barn, I really dig rock!" Fred said, bouncing in his seat.

"Me too. For a living!" laughed Barney. He rumpled up Fred's hair, annoying him. "Sorry, Fred. I'm so excited. I'm going to be a father!" Barney paused for a moment. "And we owe it all to you. Betty and I never would have been able to adopt without the money you gave us." Fred smiled. But deep down he was nervous. He hadn't told Wilma about giving Barney the money.

"Wilmaaaaa! I'm home!" shouted Fred, stepping into his house. And before he could even put his lunchbox down, Dino was all over him. "No! No! Bad boy!" he yelled, trying to get away from Dino's big wet tongue.

"Fred, do you have to get Dino so wound up when you come home?" asked Wilma, walking into the room. Pebbles giggled. Fred gave them both a kiss and settled into his Bark-o'-Lounger chair. It felt good to relax.

He didn't relax for long. The Flintstones' Pigasaurus garbage disposal was not working properly. So Wilma had gone to buy a new one. But the money had disappeared from their savings account!

"Fred, do you have any idea why there's no money in our account?" she asked him.

But Fred ignored her and headed for the kitchen. "All right, you, say 'ahhhh,'" he told the Pigasaurus. Reaching in his hand, he pulled out a slimy, bent-up fork. The Pigasaurus coughed in relief.

Wilma was upset. "Fred, we scrimped and saved for that money. And you go out and blow it on some hair-brained scheme."

"I gave our money to Barney," Fred said, closing his eyes.

"Fred Flintstone…." Wilma said, her voice rising. She stamped her foot.

"Wilma, without the money they wouldn't be able to adopt a baby."

After catching her breath, Wilma put her hands in Fred's. She stared into his eyes. "What you did was the sweetest, most generous thing I've ever heard."

After many hopes and dreams, it was finally the day the Rubbles had been waiting for. It was the day they were going to adopt a little boy. Fred, Wilma, and Pebbles had all come along. Excited—and a little bit scared, too—everyone sat in the waiting room of the Bedrock Adoption Agency.

"Okay, Mommy, Daddy…" said Mrs. Pyrite, the head of the agency. In her arms was a tiny bundle. But it wasn't a baby boy. Instead, it was a baby ape! This baby belonged to another family. Mrs. Pyrite went into the back room.

"Mr. and Mrs. Rubble, <u>this</u> is your son," she said, presenting them with a wild-looking little boy. His long hair was tangled in knots, and he was covered with dirt. In his hand was a tiny club.

"Oh Barney, isn't he precious?" sighed Betty. "Does he have a name?"

"Bamm-Bamm," Mrs. Pyrite informed them. "He was raised by wild mastodons." Wild mastodons! The Rubbles were determined to give him a good home.

Just as Bamm-Bamm made his way toward his new family, Wilma took out her camera. Flash! The light scared Bamm-Bamm. Clubbing Barney in the stomach, Bamm-Bamm jumped out of the window and ran off down the street. Drivers slammed on their feet to avoid hitting him! The Rubbles and Flintstones were in hot pursuit.

Thank goodness they caught him. Not only were there lots of changes for the Rubbles, there were lots of changes for Bamm-Bamm, too. He had his first bath. And his first haircut. He wore clothes for the first time. But best of all, Bamm-Bamm found a new friend...Pebbles.

A few nights later the Inter-Lodge Championship was held at the Bedrock Bowl-O-Rama. Fred and Barney's team, the Water Buffalos, was up against the Missing Links.

"Okay, Brother Flintstone, we need a strike to win!" Barney said excitedly. "Can you do it?"

Fred rolled his eyes. "Hey, is the earth flat?" he said confidently. He took careful aim. He rolled the ball. KABOOM! The ball smashed into the pins. The Water Buffalos won!

After doing their traditional celebration chant, the team shared a giant tub of lava juice. "I'd like to propose a toast," declared Barney. "To not only a great bowler, but a great human being. I owe my son to Fred, and I vow I'll pay him back someday, somehow."

"That was beautiful, Barney," said Fred, his voice choked up with emotion. And together, they dunked their heads into the tub.

Fred was having such a good time with his buddies, that he ended up staying out a little later than he'd planned. Trying to be quiet, he carefully tiptoed through the house. CRASH! Pebbles had left one of her toys on the floor. With a giant thud, Fred landed flat on his back.

"Look at him. Drunk as a skunkasaurus." It was Pearl, Wilma's mother—and one of Fred's worst nightmares.

Wilma hurried in and began helping Fred up. "What's that old fossil doing here?" he asked.

"Looking after my daughter and grandchild while you're out with a bunch of Neanderthals," huffed Pearl, shaking her fist at Fred.

"Oh really?" said Fred in his most insulting voice. "For your information, the lodge no longer accepts Neanderthals!"

"Enough!" Wilma exclaimed. It was no fun to hear them argue.

"You know, Wilma, you could've married Elliot Firestone, the man who invented the wheel," said Pearl, shaking her head. "But instead, you picked Fred Flintstone, the man who invented the excuse!"

"I'll show her," vowed Fred. "I'll show everybody!"

The workers at Slate and Co. liked to eat outside. Today their lunch was interrupted by Cliff Vandercave.

"I'm here to announce the Slate and Co. Executive Placement Program," he told them. "This Saturday a test will be given to determine who will be our new Junior Vice President."

A lightbulb went off in Fred's head. This was his chance to be somebody!

Fred and Barney arrived bright and early on the day of the test.

"How am I gonna compete with guys like this?" Fred asked Barney worriedly. "I'm not the executive type. My father was a quarryman and my grandfather was a quarryman...and his grandfather was an amoeba!"

To calm Fred down, Barney decided to stay and take the test with him.

"You will have one hour to complete the exam. Please carve all answers with a well-sharpened number two chisel," Cliff told the test-takers.

"Chisels down!" called Cliff after exactly one hour. Poor Fred tried to chisel in a few more answers. He knew he hadn't done well. As Barney turned in the test tablets, he saw that Fred's test had many mistakes. Barney remembered his promise to pay Fred back for the adoption money. This could be the way! Glancing around the room, Barney quickly switched his test with Fred's.

"The test results are in," announced Cliff to the crowd. "The new Junior Vice President is...Mr. Fred Flintstone."

Fred couldn't believe it. He leaped into the air, clicking his heels together. "YABBA-DABBA-DOO!"

Smiling to himself, Barney gave Fred a congratulatory hug. He had found a way to pay Fred back.

"Well, what do you think?" Fred asked Wilma, Pebbles, and Dino. It was Fred's first day on his new job. His hair was slicked back, his hands were clean, and he had on a brand-new suit.

"Daddy pretty," laughed Pebbles. Wilma and Dino looked at Fred adoringly.

"So, Fred, what do I call you now? Mr. Flintstone? Sir?" Barney asked, tipping his hard hat.

"Nah…a simple Your Highness will do," Fred joked. The two friends laughed. "No, Barney, I'm not going to be one of those guys who makes it and then forgets where he came from. First thing I'm gonna do is get everyone some vacation time. And then maybe a health plan with free foot care."

"You know what I wish you could get for us?" Barney asked. "Call it a dream. I wish we could have those little packets of ketchup in the lunchroom."

"Hey, I'm just one man," replied Fred. And then they arrived at the quarry.

"Go get 'em, big guy," said Barney, giving Fred a pat on the back. And with that, Fred proudly headed off into the offices of Slate and Co.

Cliff gave Fred a phony warm welcome, and led him down the hallway to his big new office. His pretty secretary, Miss Stone, was there to greet him.

"Mr. Flintstone, I just want you to know I enjoy working long hours, late nights, even weekends," she said in a deep voice before leaving the room.

Finally alone, Fred relaxed, putting his feet up on his desk. He pretended to dictate a memo. "Executively yours, Fred Fliiiiiiahhhh..." he yelled, flipping backward in his chair.

"Are there six or seven *i*'s in 'Fliiiiiiahhhh'?" inquired a snippy voice. It was the Dictabird. Fred stood up and stared.

It was hard to believe that yesterday he was a rock digger. Today he had his own office, his own desk...and his very own Dictabird!

"Fred is the greatest bowler on earth," Fred announced.

"Fred is the greatest bowler on earth," repeated the Dictabird. It was getting a bit tired of Fred's fooling around.

Just then, Cliff strutted into the office. "So, Flintstone, ready for your first executive action?"

"Ready and willing," said Fred, full of enthusiasm.

"Good. I want you to fire Bernard Rubble," Cliff told him.

Fire Barney! That was one thing that Fred just couldn't do.

"He scored the lowest on the test. We can't afford to keep him around. Look, Flintstone, if you don't fire him, I will."

It was a long drive home that night. Fred didn't know how he was going to break the news to Barney. But before he could come up with an explanation, they arrived at the Flintstones' house…and a surprise party! Friends from far and near had gathered to congratulate Fred on his new promotion.

"This is all Betty and Barney's doing," Wilma told Fred, placing a bright party hat on his head. "Aren't we lucky to have friends like them?"

Ohhh! This was only making things worse for Fred.

"There he is! There's my big, handsome son-in-law!" Pearl announced grandly, throwing her arms around Fred. She had had a change of heart toward him. "Why is a nobody like you sitting when a man of his stature is standing?" she yelled at a bewildered party guest. "Get up!" Pearl shoved him off his seat.

Barney stood up to give a speech—and to present Fred with a lovely briefcase. Fred refused to accept it. "You can't afford it, Barney," Fred told him glumly. "You're fired!" And with that, Fred ran out of the room. Barney trotted after him.

"Don't worry about me, Fred," he said, trying to console him. "But I gotta know. Why?" Fred told him that he had the lowest score on the test. Now Barney realized that switching the tests to help Fred cost him his own job.

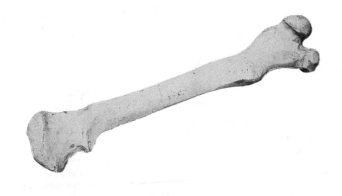

At an early morning meeting at Slate and Co., Cliff announced a new idea—steam-powered conveyor belts to move the boulders from place to place. On the conference room table was a model of what the new system would look like. Tiny boulders shot out of a small catapult and landed on conveyor belts. As Mr. Slate and his workers applauded, Fred voiced his opinion.

"There's no way this little doodad is going to do the job," he said firmly, pointing to the catapult. But everyone just laughed—and no one listened.

That afternoon, Wilma, Betty, and the kids went on a shopping trip. While Wilma tried on a fancy dress, Bamm-Bamm disappeared. Soon there was a crash—and Bamm-Bamm was found. Betty handed her credit card to the store manager to pay for damages, and he told her that the card was no longer any good. Wilma paid for everything.

They headed over to a nearby park. As Pebbles and Bamm-Bamm played, Betty tearfully confessed, "We've nearly spent all our savings. What if the adoption agency finds out?" Wilma hugged her friend. She'd always be there for her.

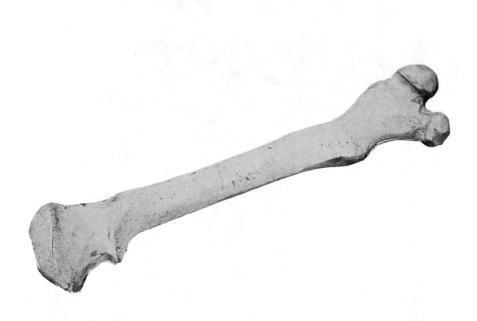

Back at Slate and Co., Fred was starting to feel at home. He had been very busy lately, chiseling his signature.

"You know, I've been signing stacks of these things for weeks now.... What are they?" he asked Miss Stone.

"Oh, just silly little forms so we can pay the contractors," she told him, sitting down on his desk. But that wasn't the truth. The forms were really firing notices for all of Fred's friends!

Suddenly, the Dictabird cleared its throat...and Fred looked up to see an annoyed Wilma in the doorway. She held Pebbles in her arms. Frowning, Wilma waited until Miss Stone left the room. She had come to talk to Fred about the Rubbles. Barney hadn't found a job, and they had had to rent out their house to make ends meet. Where were the Rubbles going to stay, Fred wondered. Wilma smiled. She knew just the place.

"How about this? The Flintstones and the Rubbles under one roof," said Fred, flipping a huge bronto steak.

"You know, Fred, it's just temporary," Barney reminded him.

"It better be!" Fred laughed, and slapped Barney on the back. Barney tried to smile, but it wasn't easy.

Inside, Betty and Wilma were busily tossing a salad. Or trying to. Each of them had her <u>own</u> idea of how it should be done. And Pebbles and Bamm-Bamm were fighting. What was happening to everybody?

The executive life wasn't all it was cracked up to be. In fact, Fred was a little bored. He missed being with his friends, missed being outside. Strolling into the conference room one afternoon, Fred picked up a tiny boulder from the model of the new quarry, and loaded the catapult. Whoops! The boulder smashed into the model, instead of landing on a conveyor belt.

"What happened here?" asked Miss Stone, running in. "Never mind. I'll get someone to fix it," she said.

"Wait," said Fred. "I don't pretend to understand it all, but won't this thing put a lot of people out of work?" he asked. Miss Stone pretended not to know. But deep in her heart, she knew Fred was right.

Fred's new job didn't give him much satisfaction. But it did give him one thing. Money. He was earning more sand dollars in a day than he'd earned in a whole week as a quarryman. The Flintstones were in the lap of luxury. They installed a pool and redecorated their house. Wilma began wearing fancy pearls and sported a new hairdo. Pebbles had more toys than she could ever play with. And Fred bought a beautiful new car, a Le Sabertooth 5000.

"Who said money doesn't buy happiness?" Fred asked Wilma, grinning from ear to ear.

Wilma was not so sure. "Isn't this too much too fast?" she wondered aloud.

Fred shook his head. "Wilma, in the buffet of life, there's no second helpings." And with that, Fred gave Wilma a big kiss.

Life was not so easy for the Rubbles.

"You know, honey, life's funny." Betty sighed. "One minute people are your best friends, then....The Flintstones have changed, Barney. I hardly know them since Fred became such a big shot."

Barney didn't have much to say. All he could think of was that <u>he</u> should be the one driving a new car, wearing new clothes, drinking pineapple passion punch. If only he hadn't switched the tests....

A few days later, the Flintstones were treating the Rubbles to a fancy dinner at Cavern on the Green. Before Fred left the office, Cliff dropped off some tablets for him to chisel. The tablets would authorize some time off for the workers, Cliff told him.

After Cliff left, the Dictabird walked across Fred's desk. "Just a moment," it said. "Only an idiot signs something before reading it."

"Excuse me, I'm the executive and you're the office equipment," Fred replied coldly. He couldn't be bothered to read the tablets. He didn't want to miss one minute of his night on the town.

It was getting late, and Barney still hadn't arrived at Cavern on the Green. Fred and Wilma were dancing up a storm on the restaurant's dance floor. Betty sat alone at a table, waiting patiently. As the Flintstones returned to their seats, Fred accidentally knocked a glass of water over. A busboy scurried over to clean it up, and a look of recognition spread across Fred's face.

"Barney? You're a busboy?!"

Barney nodded. "And I don't have to fight Dino for my supper." He quickly yanked the wet tablecloth off and walked away.

Just then, a news bulletin blared from a TV in the corner. "The demonstration continues to get uglier here at Slate and Co., following the unexpected layoff of almost everyone," said the reporter on the screen.

Barney ran back to the table. "Do you know what happened to everyone at the quarry today?" he yelled.

"I oughtta. It was my idea. I sent them all off on a nice long vacation," Fred said proudly.

"A permanent vacation," Barney said angrily. "You fired them!"

"I didn't do that," stammered Fred. He and Wilma were both stunned.

"Yes, you did. Fred, the only reason you got that job is because I switched tests with you!" exploded Barney.

"This has gone far enough," Wilma said. "After everything we've done for you…"

"You used to be such nice people," interrupted Betty. "But now you're just rich snobs." Betty grabbed Barney's hand, and they headed for the door.

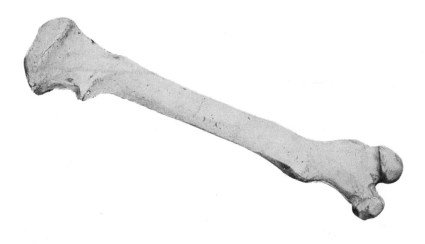

Later that night, the Rubbles moved all of their things out of the Flintstones' house. Wilma couldn't stand it.

"Fred, say something," she pleaded. "Aren't you the least bit sorry?"

"You bet I'm sorry—sorry that I ever met the little moocher!" Fred answered angrily. "Who needs the Rubbles?"

"I do!" cried out Wilma. "But what I don't need is this necklace...or this lamp...or the TV..." Wilma threw all of their new things onto the floor. Fred couldn't believe it. He'd never seen Wilma so angry. Dishes were flying, lamps were breaking. Dino hid under the sink with the Pigasaurus.

A few moments later, Wilma, in her old clothes, headed out the door. She was on her way to Pearl's. And Dino and Pebbles were with her.

"Wait...." called Fred. But his words were lost in the wind.

The next day Fred stormed into his office. One by one, he went through the files. He threw the tablets onto his desk.

"I'm onto your little scam," he told Cliff and Miss Stone as they barged into the room. "You've been stealing money from the company."

"Well, it's your signature on all the forms," Cliff replied.

"I'm innocent!" cried Fred.

"Doesn't look that way. Look at you. New clothes, fancy furniture...even a new car," Cliff said.

Fred had been framed! As Cliff called security, Fred hurried out of the room. There must be something he could do to prove his innocence. But what?

Wilma, Pebbles, and Dino returned home. And Pearl joined them. They were very worried. Fred had been missing for two days. He was wanted by the police!

After seeing Fred on "Bedrock's Most Wanted," Betty and Bamm-Bamm arrived at the Flintstones'.

"I just couldn't let you go through this alone," Betty said.

"Fred might be a lot of things, but he's not a thief," Wilma declared. And she had just thought of a way to prove it. Leaving Pearl in charge, Wilma and Betty headed off into the dark and rainy streets of Bedrock.

Wilma and Betty tricked the guard at the Slate and Co. building. Then they slipped inside and found Fred's office.

"Come on, wake up," Wilma whispered to the Dictabird, snapping her fingers. "You're the only one who can clear my husband."

But the Dictabird stuck out its tongue and went back to sleep. Betty had no patience for that kind of behavior. She grabbed the Dictabird by the throat, and she and Wilma ran out of the building.

At that very moment, Cliff and Miss Stone were taking hundreds of sand dollars from the office safe. Everything was all set. Then Cliff saw Wilma and Betty running from the building. They had the Dictabird!

"Son of a brachiosaurus!" shouted Cliff, running out after them.

Cliff wasn't the only one running. Fred was being chased by an angry mob. He was wearing a disguise, but that didn't stop him from being recognized. Turning the corner, he ran straight into another mob! There was nowhere left to run.

"Stone him! Call him names!" howled the angry crowd. Just as they were about to tie Fred up to a tree, soft music drifted through the air. A large white truck pulled up to the crowd.

"Anybody want a sno-cone?" It was Barney! He had arrived in the nick of time. But the crowd didn't want to listen to him. They started to tie him up, too.

"I thought you came to save me!" cried Fred.

"Save you? I saw a crowd. I figured I could sell a few sno-cones," Barney replied. He still hadn't forgiven Fred for his remarks in the restaurant.

"Look, Barn, I know you're a little mad at me, but if I have to have someone hanging beside me, I'm glad it's you," Fred said softly.

Barney shrugged his shoulders. "I'm a loser," he said.

"No, you're not. You're the best friend a guy ever had," Fred told him. And he meant it. Straining against the ropes, they shook pinkies.

CRASH! A car had driven into the tree, knocking it over. Out leaped Betty and Wilma. They perched the Dictabird on a boulder.

"Everybody, listen to him," Wilma shouted to the crowd. But the Dictabird didn't want to speak. It wanted an apology from Fred.

"You hurt my feelings, Mr. Flintstone, treating me as if I were an ordinary piece of office equipment," said the Dictabird, blinking its eyes. Grumbling, Fred finally apologized…and the Dictabird began to tell what it knew.

After all the commotion, the Rubbles and the Flintstones headed for home. The Flintstones' house was a mess. Furniture was upside down. Vases were smashed. And Dino and Pearl were tied up.

"Pebbles and Bamm-Bamm are gone!" shrieked Wilma, running out of Pebbles' room. She had a note in her hand. It read:

If you want to see your kids again, bring the Dictabird to the quarry at dawn. No police.

The frightened families stared at each other. It would be a long wait until dawn.

As the sun rose over the town of Bedrock, Fred, Barney, and the Dictabird arrived at the quarry. Cliff stood beside a catapult, his hand on the power switch. The catapult was used to shoot boulders onto a conveyor belt. Then they would move ahead to a giant rock slicer. But now there weren't just boulders on the belt. Bamm-Bamm and Pebbles were there, too!

Fred promptly handed the Dictabird over, but Cliff turned on the power anyway. The conveyor belt began to move. Barney ran toward the children. Scrambling up to reach them, he hit his head on the machine. He was out like a light. Now it was all up to Fred to save them. But how? Suddenly Fred remembered the mini catapult in the conference room. There <u>was</u> something he could do.

Groaning under the pressure, Fred pushed the catapult into a new position. Pipes began to burst. Steam and smoke filled the air. Pebbles and Bamm-Bamm were crying.

Meanwhile, Miss Stone had shown up. She realized what she and Cliff were doing was wrong, and she had come to help. As Cliff struggled with the Dictabird, Miss Stone hit Cliff over the head with a bag of sand dollars. Crossing their fingers, Miss Stone and the Dictabird watched Fred.

He fired off a boulder from the catapult. Up, up, up it went…until SMASH! The boulder crashed into the machine. Water and crushed rocks came spilling out. The machine was destroyed. At that moment, Barney came to, grabbed the kids, and jumped to safety.

"YABBA-DABBA-DOO!" shouted Fred, leaping into the air. Miss Stone and the Dictabird hugged each other.

Stumbling up from the ground, Cliff tried to get away. Fred wasn't about to let that happen. He threw a boulder straight at him.

"Steeeerike!" Fred exclaimed as the boulder knocked Cliff over and into the water and crushed rock.

Siren birds blared as the police, with Wilma, Betty, and Mr. Slate close behind, arrived at the scene.

"How did this happen?" asked Mr. Slate. He gestured to Cliff. The powdered rocks and water had covered him. He was frozen like a statue.

"Well, the machine went nuts…and the crushed-up rocks mixed with water…and…I'm really sorry," mumbled Fred.

"Sorry? I <u>love</u> it! You're a genius!"

"Huh?" said Fred, puzzled.

"Thanks to you, the Stone Age is over. I'm naming this stuff after my daughter, Concretia," said Mr. Slate excitedly. "Hire everybody back. You're our new President of the Concrete Division!"

But this was one offer Fred had to refuse. "All my life I wanted to be somebody. When it happened, I became somebody I didn't like," he explained. And even though the new job would make him richer, he didn't care. He had something that all the sand dollars in the world couldn't buy. Wilma and Pebbles and Dino...and the best friends in the world...Betty and Barney.

"I would like a few things, though," Fred said. "Vacations for everybody. And, most importantly, those little packets of ketchup in the lunchroom."

"Done!" replied Mr. Slate. He waved as everyone trooped off for the Flintmobile.

"Fred, I'm so proud of you," said Wilma.

"And I'm proud of you," Betty told Barney, squeezing his arm.

Fred and Barney grinned. These two old friends had a lot to be happy about. They had their old jobs back. They had the most wonderful families. And, best of all, they had each other.

The End